Without Dad

Written and Illustrated

By

Linda Austin Rutledge

© 2002 by Linda Austin Rutledge.
All rights reserved.

No part of this book may be reproduced,
stored in a retrieval system, or transmitted by any
means, electronic, mechanical, photocopying,
recording, or otherwise, without written
permission from the author.

ISBN: 0-7596-8625-4 (Electronic)
ISBN: 0-7596-8626-2 (Softcover)
ISBN: 1-4033-3653-9 (Hardcover)

This book is printed on acid free paper.

1stBooks - rev. 05/22/02

This book is written for all growing up
without a Dad

Enjoy the days upon this earth,
All you without your Dads,
Let no sadness of yesterday
Disturb the love you have.
Don't worry about tomorrow
With thoughts of coming fear,
Your Dad will be your changeless man,
His life has brought you here.

Linda Austin Rutledge

WITHOUT DAD

By Linda Austin Rutledge

Growing up in Michigan was to me the best place in the world. As a child I would wonder why God chose this place for me. To me a childhood in Michigan was like heaven. The winters were cold and snow blown; the lake would freeze to form perfect ice-skating rinks. Spring was filled with wildflowers and newborn animals. During the summer I would lay in the yard with the sun baking me brown and watch the butterfly's, listening to the drone of the bees flying from flower to flower. The fall we were usually knee deep in leaves that needed raking and a garden full of vegetables that needed to be picked and canned.

I have never left Michigan and have no desire to do so. Florida seems to call a lot of people and many move there. I could never imagine not having the four seasons that I have grown to love. Just when we tire of the deep snowfall, spring arrives with its newness, then summer with all its heat and sunshine, just as we tire of the heat fall is upon us and then the wonder of winter. Christmas would not be the same for me if it did not snow.

That is always the first thing I hope for is snow before Christmas. Not just a little but a good storm that frosts all the windows and drifts over everything.

Living within walking distance to Lake Erie just added to the enjoyment of the land. The most memorable experiences were ice-skating across the frozen great lake. The cracking of the ice sent chills down my spine and the wind blew so fast across the frozen ice it whistled. I could skate for miles and never stop.

The small township of LaSalle was mostly made of family and friends. As kids we were taught to wave at every car that drove by because we knew everyone, and if one was a stranger we welcomed them to our world.

Without Dad
Written and Illustrated by Linda Austin Rutledge

MY BEGINNINGS

Linda Austin Rutledge

Without Dad
Written and Illustrated by Linda Austin Rutledge

My beginnings

1

I, was born Linda Kay Austin July 8 in Monroe, Michigan Mercy Hospital to Arthur and Sally Austin. She was a homemaker and he was a sheep farmer and worked as a controller at Gordon Mfg. The story goes that Grandpa Austin (an English gentlemen) could not keep his 3 boys in line so he moved from Royal Oak and bought a farm in LaSalle and started a sheep farm.

I am not sure that my Dad was the problem as he was a banker in Royal Oak according to the Newspaper. But my uncles were a handful I am sure as both Ed and Wilbur (Fats) as he was nicknamed were heavy drinkers. Fats was skinny as a rail and I always wondered where he found his nickname. Dad also had two sisters.

I had an older sister Delores with beautiful red hair and an older brother William (Bill) who also had red hair. My mother must have been thrilled to have a blonde because as long as I could remember she would rinse my hair with lemon juice after the shampoo to keep it light. Red hair was a family trait on her family side and they all seemed pretty proud of it. My mother also had beautiful red hair.

My Dad had just cleared two acres out of my Grandfather Austin's woods on LaPlaisance Road and built a small home. It only had 2 bedrooms upstairs and I think his plans were to increase the size later but he never had the chance. Dad also raised chickens for eggs and had a cow for milk. One evening during a bad storm lighting struck the three next to the cow and shed and burned down the shed killing the cow. The chickens were raised many years more.

Dad was a very good artist, and was hired to do the cover illustrations for a sport magazine just before he died. Dad died when I was only a toddler and I never really knew him, only by stories people told. He must have been a very talented and intelligent man as he was in the process of running electricity through the woods to build subdivision. Dad also built our home single-handed and it is still a solid house many years later.

My mother's family came from Napoleon Ohio and are of Irish descendants. She was born in Napoleon to a family with 11 children. Most with the same red hair she had. They moved to S. Dixie Hwy, Monroe and Grandpa Green started a furniture repair shop on West Front St. Downtown. Mom was a twin Louella and she was named Marcella. Later her nickname was Sally. She also was in her day intelligent and graduated from St.

Without Dad
Written and Illustrated by Linda Austin Rutledge

Marys School. Then went on to the Monroe Business Academy.

Linda Austin Rutledge

Without Dad
Written and Illustrated by Linda Austin Rutledge

EARLY MEMORIES AS A CHILD

Linda Austin Rutledge

Without Dad
Written and Illustrated by Linda Austin Rutledge

Early memories as a child

2

When I was around a year old my Dad has a mole removed and died a few months later. Grandma Austin said when she would cut his hair that sometimes she would accidentally cut the mole off. I am sure that did not help the situation. My mother was pregnant and had three little ones; I sometimes wondered how she survived. After Dad died she gave birth to my brother and named him Arthur Austin Jr. He remained living at home the rest of his life almost as a replacement. At the time it must have been very heartbreaking to give birth to a son of your lost husband. But I think it was a gift from God. He left only to attend College for his degree, taking care of the house and yard that my father cleared for years to come

We had a wonderful childhood growing up in the country, we missed having a Dad but life went on. The closest neighbors were mostly our cousins and aunts and uncles. LaPlaisance Road in LaSalle was a very secluded farming area. The closest homes we could walk to were our cousins. I was the only girl except for my older sister and she had a friend her age that she spent most of her time with. My sister was five years older and was far more grown up than I could ever be. Her friend lived a little down the road and they visited each other, leaving me with the boys. Growing up with the boys I learned to hunt, fish and shoot a bow and arrow with the best. I was to say the least a Tomboy. I could hold my own with any of the boys.

The gang consisted of my brothers, my three cousins Lloyd and Ron and Gary and a boy nick named Buzzy, who was of no relation but lived with his grandfather Pippi, owner of a local greenhouse. We were quite a crew. The best quality it left me with was the ability to get along with boys. Many years later I worked as a representative with a group of over 20 men and to this day they still are my friends. My cousins all treated me like a sister and I never really felt alone as I was always with the boys.

The childhood tales of the cousins and I are wild and fun I would like to share some of them, they are all true and funny now that I look back at them. I often wonder how we did so much without getting in trouble. As a child I was never spanked in my entire life. Once my Uncle Jim heard that and gave me a few whacks just kidding around, so I would know what a spanking was. He was my mother's brother and one of my favorite Uncles. I

Without Dad
Written and Illustrated by Linda Austin Rutledge

think he always tried to take the place of my Dad. He would tease me that he was going to give me a bowl of mouse soup to which I would scream and run. He nicknamed me Zinnia for some unknown reason.

Linda Austin Rutledge

Without Dad
Written and Illustrated by Linda Austin Rutledge

ROUTINE OF LIFE

Linda Austin Rutledge

Without Dad
Written and Illustrated by Linda Austin Rutledge

Routine of life

3

On Saturday night we always had to be clean for church on Sunday, so the bath was scheduled to start right after supper. My father had a great house plan but because he passed away so early in his life at the age of 34. We had a big bathtub and bathroom but no plumbing to it so we had to heat water and fill a large tub in the kitchen. There was one rule that the cleanest went first. This was a good lesson to try to be clean at the end of the week. As kids we took for granted the routine, but to this day I wonder why the hot water wasn't carried to the brand new tub in the bathroom.

My mother was a very creative woman, she could do anything from repairing a roof to fixing a car. During the years growing up we all learned to be very independent. She set the example, living without a husband she learned the hard way how to do it all. Never dating or getting married again she was the most independent woman I ever knew.

She worked hard and always had a hot meal for us at the end of the day. She was never one to tell us she loved us but we all knew that she loved us more than anything on earth. I think all four of us turned out to be very successful human beings, mostly due to my mother's influence, I always wondered what our lives would have been like had Dad lived.

When my mother first went back to work she had to leave my brother Art and I at Grandma Greens. There we were rocked to sleep and taken care of by her. I was only four but I have vivid memories of Grandma Green holding me tight to her and rocking me, I remember not liking the rocking because she would hold me tight to here arm pit which had a strong odor. My brother Art at age three left Grandmas one day and walked about two miles to a general store in LaSalle to where mom worked. I guess Grandma must have been to busy rocking me to notice he left.

Tragically at the age of seven my brother Bill was struck with polio. As if life did not deal us enough he was left paralyzed. They told us he would never walk again. As I said mom raised independent kids. He not only walked, ran and even learned to ride a bike. He was left with a brace on his right leg but made up his mind to have a regular life and he did.

All in all I feel the tough life we had made us much stronger than other children. If we had been raised without any hard times we most likely would have turned out to be entirely different

Without Dad
Written and Illustrated by Linda Austin Rutledge

people than we are today. I was always thankful for all I received and never would have inflicted pain on anyone because I knew first hand what real pain was.

Linda Austin Rutledge

Without Dad
Written and Illustrated by Linda Austin Rutledge

SCHOOL DAYS

Linda Austin Rutledge

Without Dad
Written and Illustrated by Linda Austin Rutledge

School Days

4

My earliest memories of school was hiding under my desk so the teacher would not call on me I was extremely shy. I went to Avalon School which was a one room school on LaPlaisance Road about one mile from our home. Kindergarten consisted of two children myself and a girl named Ellen. I had my choice at noon to either walk home by myself or stay on the playground and play until my brother and sister finished the day.

Some days I stayed and some days I walked home. The road in our neighborhood was safe in those days. I had two great barriers to pass on the way home. First one was the Luft farm dogs, they scared the daylights out of me never really chasing me but standing in their yard barking and acting like they were going to take my life.

The second barrier to pass was the Krueger farm. Grandma Krueger (my cousin's grandmother) and her sister Aunt Elise were without a doubt the best cooks in LaSalle. They made sugar cookies the size of a saucer. To top it off they loved us kids. In our neighborhood all kids belonged to everyone. We were welcomed everywhere. Well I generally would stop at Kruegers for one of their sugar cookies, sitting on their screened in porch I would savor every bite. They would also let me gather eggs in the chicken coop and help them bake the sugar cookies. Sometimes there would be a dish of ice-cream to eat and then I would sit in their parlor and listen to the soaps on the radio with them. It was a daily routine for them and I loved being part of it. I don't remember ever listening to the soaps but watching their reactions and wondering how a program could bring tears to their eyes. They had great hollyhocks along the garage and I could sit out beside the creek and make beautiful dolls out of the blossoms. Life couldn't get any better than that but I did worry my mom when I was late.

I am still amazed that a five-year-old would walk a mile home alone. But we had no fear in a neighborhood of relatives. Someone was always looking out for us. The next year Avalon school was moved and the I-75 expressway was built, where it stood. I then went on to LaSalle School and then the next year Custer School was built and I was driven to school by bus.

I had a variety of wonderful bus drivers but the bus ride never came close to the great time I had walking home. The bus never provided me with sugar cookies or ice cream, and never listened to

Without Dad
Written and Illustrated by Linda Austin Rutledge

soap operas on the bus radio. Those days were over. Mom never understood why I did not enjoy riding in a bright yellow bus rather than walking. It was a kid thing I guess.

Linda Austin Rutledge

Without Dad
Written and Illustrated by Linda Austin Rutledge

TALENT AND TOYS

Linda Austin Rutledge

Talent and Toys

5

As early as I can remember, I loved to draw and paint. My mother could not draw a straight line and we always wondered where the talent came from. One day my brother and I were exploring and we came across a beautiful pencil sketch of wild pheasants on the drywall of a small closet. We found that our Dad had drawn it. I could visualize him when he would tire of building the house lying back and relaxing while sketching a picture. We then realized where we inherited the talent from our Dad not our Mom.

My mothers Sister Norma, must have seen the talent I had and encouraged me by buying me gifts of sketch pads and oil paints. Every Christmas I knew I would get something to help me out with my hobby. Her belief in me made me keep on with it and to this day I enjoy painting.

If nothing else being into art makes you more aware of everything around you. It has always been impossible for me to pass by anything without looking for beauty. Every sunrise and sunset is a potential painting in my eyes.

Creativity abounded, I loved crafts, knitting, sewing, sketching, crocheting, you name it I did it. I would tackle anything not always with great results but I sure had a good time doing it. As young children we never had the many toys like most other children, this lead to developing talents and creating our own entertainment. My favorite toys were Jacks, for some unknown reason I would sit for hours on the dining-room hardwood floors and play jacks. I loved my dolls but with the boys it was not something we could play together. We were all too competitive to play many games, as we all wanted to win. Monopoly usually ended with the Banker closing the bank and keeping all the money. We also were too active and could not sit still for the amount of time most games took.

Amazingly we were the first family to get a Television, as mom won it at a local store contest. We went from sitting around the radio in the evening to sitting around the Television. A rule was laid down my mom however, never turn the set on during daylight. She was always great at sending us outside to get fresh air.

The most important treasure we had was our own bike, given to us by various relatives and neighbors as they grew out of them. We logged many miles on those bikes in the summer months. Whichever cousins woke up first would hop on the

Without Dad
Written and Illustrated by Linda Austin Rutledge

bikes and head to whoever wasn't there. Mostly our yard was the meeting place. We would plan our day under the thornapple tree.

Linda Austin Rutledge

Without Dad
Written and Illustrated by Linda Austin Rutledge

THE ORCHARD

Linda Austin Rutledge

Without Dad
Written and Illustrated by Linda Austin Rutledge

The Orchard

6

Many days were spent in Kruegers orchard. It was full of apple trees of all kinds. When we were very little we were allowed to walk to the (first gate) the orchard started there. As we grew older we were then allowed to walk to the corner, on the corner were our cousin's homes. It never occurred to us to disobey our mother, when she set our limitations to the first gate we knew in time that we would be allowed to travel further. She had a reason for all her rules and we never questioned them. Well my first memories were of the orchard. My favorite was green apples, with salt and I would climb a tree and sit for hours eating green apples with my salt shaker. Later in the evening I would always end up with a sick stomach but it never stopped me from enjoying those beautiful apples.

Kruegers had many cows that they would let graze in the orchard and I would never go in the orchard when they were out. One bull was especially mean and would lower his head and chase anything. One hot sunny day I went to the orchard in the morning to have my favorite green apple and while up in the tree the cows were let out. The bull of course ended up right below me. There was no place to go but sit tight. Now I am not sure to this day that the bull would actually have harmed me but I did not find out. I sat in the apple tree for hours and hours. Later in the day when it started getting hot they left for the barn and I escaped. I had been alone as none of the other kids liked green apples.

Our next brush with a cow was fishing on Otter Creek. It was a cool summer night, my brothers and I decided to fish with flashlights. We went down to the Knab Road Bridge and were enjoying the fishing when out of the brush came a huge charging (bear). We all took off to the nearest house and reported the bear. When the neighbor came back to help us find it he found instead a large cow that had gotten loose.

From that day on I had no affection for cows or bulls. The bear story was never repeated to the cousins, and my brothers never admitted to seeing a bear, even though they ran ahead of me shouting "it's a bear- it's a bear." Year's later Bill still raises cows of course he did not live through the orchard incident as I had. He even has an orchard at his place and lets the cows graze in it. I just hope no one there eats green apples.

Without Dad
Written and Illustrated by Linda Austin Rutledge

Part of the old orchard is still there but cousins Lloyd and Ron built their homes in it and took most of the trees down. I still am reminded, of all the fun I had, every time I drive past what is left of the orchard.

Linda Austin Rutledge

Without Dad
Written and Illustrated by Linda Austin Rutledge

TAKING TRIPS

Linda Austin Rutledge

Without Dad
Written and Illustrated by Linda Austin Rutledge

Taking trips

7

As I was growing up I took for granted that the phone was just another way all the relatives could keep an eye on us. We had a party line consisting of my Grandmother, Aunts and Uncles. We were never alone as any given moment we could pick up the phone and "listen" to who ever was using the phone at the time. Mom told us it was wrong but curiosity would always take over. Besides we said, they all would listen to us even join in with their opinion on whatever the subject was. It wasn't until years later when I was talking to my boyfriend Larry that I realized that my Grandmother really was an embarrassment when she started quizzing us as to where we were going. What I took for granted Larry thought was strange, it made me realize that everyone must not do this.

The phone never saved us kids bike time, as I never remember using it to call any of the cousins. To this day the same rotary-dial phone hangs on my mothers dining room wall. Later it became a contact with Mom when she took a job at Mercy Hospital. For most of our lives she worked the afternoon shift from three to eleven. This way she could be home with us at night and get us up in the mornings. I remember how excited I would be on her days off when she would be home all day. Even though she had no outside friends and never as far as I can remember went anywhere without us kinds, we missed her when she was at work.

Mom's big trip's consisted of taking us with her to pick strawberries, or peaches. The peach picking trips were the best because she would drive all the way to Irish Hills to find what she considered the best and least expensive. Kruegers orchard had a few apples to eat but for mom's favorite was canning peaches. We would also visit Irish Hills Lake while we were there. We kids had the run of the orchards and I am sure we ate at least half a bushel while we were picking. We grew up on garden produce and canned vegetables and fruits. Mom was very good at gardening and must have liked weeding and hoeing as I barely remember doing much of it.

Cooking was something else I never remember doing until I was married. Mom took over all the cooking and I guess she must have enjoyed that too. We ate what we called Big Yellow pancakes all our lives only to find out later that they were called crepes. She was big on waffles too and Saturday was waffle day. I never liked to eat anything but tea and toast but she would make sure

Without Dad
Written and Illustrated by Linda Austin Rutledge

we had our fill of waffles whether we wanted them or not. I am still not a big fan of waffles.

Linda Austin Rutledge

Without Dad
Written and Illustrated by Linda Austin Rutledge

THE WOODCHUCK CREEK 4-H CLUB

Linda Austin Rutledge

Without Dad
Written and Illustrated by Linda Austin Rutledge

The Woodchuck Creek 4-H Club

8

Later on in life we decided to form a 4-H Club. The phone came in handy in calling in kids from the distant neighborhoods. We needed at least 10 members so the cousins just weren't enough.

The 4-H Club needed an adult leader and no one would volunteer. We then entered mom's name as the leader. The meeting place of course was in our front yard under the thornapple tree. The motley crew got together made up of cousins, Dusseau kids and Anteau boys. We wanted to name the club the Otter Creek Club but another group already used it. We then went to the next creek, which was named Woodchuck Creek now they call it Mortar Creek. Woodchuck Creek ran through Kruegers farm and divided LaSalle Township from Monroe Township. Well any way that is how we got such and unusual name for our club. We were the only 4-H Club in Michigan I am sure that was really run by kids.

Our meetings would start after supper and end when it got dark. We entered projects in the County Fair with some help from parents. We would sign up for projects and then beg a parent to help us. Each year when the Fair would come, our neighbor would load all the club into his grain truck. He would then drive us to the fair, let us out and pick us back up at 5:00. No 4-H official ever guessed that our club was truly run by kids.

The County Fair was the most exciting thing that happened in the summer. There we met other kids, learned how to cook, sew, make electrical cords, and bird boxes. We also picked any vegetables from the garden and entered them. For our efforts we won beautiful blue ribbons. The memories of the Fair are forever with me and I still love to visit it. Hardly anything has changed in the past years. The layout is still the same as it was. We never went on the mid-way rides mostly due to lack of money. There was a separation of the midway kids and the 4-H kids. Today it is still the same way. 4-H members all received free passes and usually there were games we could participate in with each other.

I carry found memories of the Fair. The memories cling to me long after the dust and cotton candy were washed away. The lessons that we learned in 4-H stayed with us forever, they were not forced upon us by the adult world, we choose them. My blue ribbons were carefully packed away in tissue and saved in a wooden cigar box. My 4-H pins first year and five-year were also

Without Dad
Written and Illustrated by Linda Austin Rutledge

saved. But most of all I saved the 4-H memories. I wonder to this day how we ever carried it off, not having an adult in charge. Maybe the adults knew all along and just felt sorry for a bunch of country kids without a leader.

Linda Austin Rutledge

Without Dad
Written and Illustrated by Linda Austin Rutledge

ADVENTURES ON OTTER CREEK

Linda Austin Rutledge

Without Dad
Written and Illustrated by Linda Austin Rutledge

Adventures on Otter Creek

9

We lived about a mile from Otter Creek, which was the largest creek in LaSalle Township. My first adventure was learning to swim, Mom would drive us to Lake Erie at least once a week in the summer to swim but with the waves and sandbars you never really had to swim to have a good time. Just walk out a ways and you would cool down from the heat of the day. Other times we would ride our bikes down picking up bottles to turn in at a store nearby and have a bottle of pop. Trouble with that was the bike ride back in the heat of the day defeated the cooling off.

Otter Creek taught me how to really swim or dog paddle if you want. One jump off the dock and I had to paddle as hard as I could because of the bloodsuckers. They lurked in the bottom mud of the creek and if your foot touched bottom you were bound to pick up one or two. They were the most sickening things on earth. I could not swim at all until Otter Creek. Then I could stay on top of the water for a long period of time. My brothers would jump off the railroad bridge into the creek but knowing the bottom occupants I refused, as they would always end up with mud from jumping.

Bill also wove a dip-net and we went dip netting in the creek. That was an exciting venture. Whenever the net went down we were never sure of its contents when we raised it up. Fish, crabs, snakes anything in the water was fair game. I don't ever remember doing anything with them but looking the contents over and then dropping it back.

Sometimes we would go to neighbors that lived on the creek and skate but it wasn't nearly as exciting as skating Lake Erie. We also had Woodchuck Creek to skate on and it was a very sheltered creek and much warmer without winds. I could get really into creative skating on Woodchuck Creek with no one watching. I loved the one leg spins and skating backwards which caused many spills. It was much more fun when no strangers were watching, none of the cousins laughed when you were down.

Creeks always offered us something to do, depending on the season. Everyone needs to grow up by some type of waterway. Michigan offered the most no matter where anyone lived. When I was growing up all the creeks and lakes were so clear you could see the bottom. I would lie on the bridge for hours watching all that swam past. My

Without Dad
Written and Illustrated by Linda Austin Rutledge

favorite were the frogs, it wasn't summer without the background of frogs calling to each other in the evening.

Linda Austin Rutledge

Without Dad
Written and Illustrated by Linda Austin Rutledge

THE LIBRARY

Linda Austin Rutledge

Without Dad
Written and Illustrated by Linda Austin Rutledge

The Library

10

While growing up we did not have much in the ways of extras. Mom used to drive us to the City Library in Monroe once a month on Saturday. We were in our glory when we could pick out any books and check them out for free. It was better than a candy store to us because we all loved to read. Mom would always subscribe to the Evening News and I can remember sitting on her lap with her reading me the funny section. Other than that I really don't remember her reading us anything else. At first she took us there I think to keep us occupied in the winter months. As we grew older and became bookworms, I think it backfired on her. I can remember her yelling at all of us to put down those darn books and get outside in the fresh air.

I read many books. My favorite was adventure books that would take you all over the world. They always said you cannot judge a book by its cover but I first would be drawn to the pictures on the cover and if they were illustrated right I would then read the book. The library still has the second floor children's room that I loved when I was young. Because of Mom's influence we all became very good readers. I still love a good book and belong to at least two book clubs at any given time. My library card is more important to me than any charge card I own today.

In the winter I would curl up and escape to warm summers on the prairies and in the hot summer months I would go to blizzards in the west. You could escape just about anything in a good book. I had a habit and still do to this day of picking up a book and not being able to set it down until I finished. I solved my problem with Mom by reading outside in the trees, she was happy I was in the fresh air.

One year I won a poster contest for national library week by drawing a book opening with a beautiful angel floating out of it I titled it "open a book and you will open the world." I think I took first place because of the truth in the statement not the picture.

When I read books and then later saw the movie it was always a great disappointment because I could imagine way better than they produced it. The worst I ever remember was one book I read and in my book the illustration had one picture of the girl with black curly hair and in the movie it was blonde. That detail ruined the entire movie for me. I still have that first book and I put a

Without Dad
Written and Illustrated by Linda Austin Rutledge

check on the inside cover every time I read it. It has five checks in it, I really must have liked reading that one.

Linda Austin Rutledge

Without Dad
Written and Illustrated by Linda Austin Rutledge

OUR PETS

Linda Austin Rutledge

Our Pets

11

During our childhood our lives were filled with pets of all kinds. First every spring came dogs and cats. We were in such a rural area everyone in Monroe that had a litter of kittens or puppies would dump them off. We took in everything, Mom never said no to a poor homeless dog or cat. We didn't even have to beg to keep them.

The puppies were the best, yellow, black or spotted each of us would pick our favorite and it would be ours and ours alone. Kittens were in great abundance and never seemed to last to long as the puppies loved to chase them up the trees. I think the cats left for Krueger barn where they would get a squirt of milk from who ever milked the cows.

Our dogs also chased Krueger chickens and would come home now and then with shotgun pellets in their skin. That was just the farmer's way, they never called to complain to us, just shot the dogs to chase them away. We all understood the rules. Most of the dogs would end their lives the same way they came, on the road. They all seemed to like chasing cars when they grew up.

Poor mom would have to carry them back and bury them by the apple tree. (We had a huge pet cemetery by the apple tree.)

We once took a baby fox that a farmer plowed up, the tractor ran over its mother. There were a few other babies but mom was the only one that let us keep one. We named him Cookie and he was just like a puppy until he grew older. Then every time he would play hard he smelled just like a skunk and bite much harder than any dog we ever had. Towards the fall he started a howl in the evening as if calling to other wild foxes. Then he began to leave first one night and then two. He then left to join the others and never came back. We had a good summer with him and learned a lot about wild animals.

Our next wild pet was a crow, abandoned by its mother we took him in and named him Caw. He was very demanding, living in the basement eating constantly, bread and milk and yelling at us. As soon as he could fly we let him back into the woods. The basement smelled of milk, bread and crow for many months later.

I also had a few secret pets that even my brothers did not know about. Mom had at one time found a mouse hole in the dining room and nailed a tin can top over it. I had found a tiny mouse one fall day and brought it inside to keep it warm. So

Without Dad
Written and Illustrated by Linda Austin Rutledge

that no one would find it and end his life, I opened the mouse hole and put him in. Every day I would feed it scraps of food. Now I did state that I never was spanked in my life but I am positive that I would have been punished for that pet.

Linda Austin Rutledge

Without Dad
Written and Illustrated by Linda Austin Rutledge

SPRING

Linda Austin Rutledge

Without Dad
Written and Illustrated by Linda Austin Rutledge

Spring

12

Spring always was welcome. Usually the winter was long and hard and we really missed being outside. My Dad before he died had started a flower garden full of climbing roses, lilacs, peonies, daisies, and purple butterfly flowers. They always reminded me of him when they were in bloom. Then came wild strawberries and black wild raspberries. We would put the raspberries in milk and make a purple drink that was out of this world. Tornadoes were also a sign of spring. I was the only one that ever went in the basement when the wind started howling. Everyone else was confident that the house was indestructible.

Early in the spring the local greenhouse would hire us for a short time to help plant flats of flowers and vegetables for the greenhouse. They would have great piles of dirt and we would fill the flats and plant the seeds. At Easter time they would let me help make corsages. They had yards of beautiful ribbon and buckets of flowers.

Spring also brought a variety of mushrooms in the woods. Mom would pick a basket and then fry them in butter in a skillet. We thought they were great but to this day I wonder how we didn't get poisoned as I am sure she did not know a mushroom from a toadstool. We had fried mushrooms on toast and fried mushrooms plain, anyway she cooked them, they were great.

The woods that my Dad did not clear provided us with a great playground. In the spring the entire woods was carpeted with yellow and white tiger tooth lily. I picked so many as a child I was sure they would not come back the next spring, but they did. Warm spring evenings we would play red rover, throwing a ball over the roof. When we wanted real adventure we would get out the bow and arrows and play a game of shooting an arrow straight up in the air and then running to avoid the arrow when it came shooting down. Now that I look back we must have been a little crazy to do that.

We would stay outside long past sunset just enjoying the warm evening. Sooner or later the bats would come out of the woods diving at us. That always signaled the end of the evening. I would run as fast as I could for the shelter of the house. Everyone always said bats liked to dive at your head to snatch hair. I never stayed around to see just what they were after. I was always the first one in.

Without Dad
Written and Illustrated by Linda Austin Rutledge

Spring also brought us the newborn kittens and puppies. The best days of our lives were laying in the yard with five or six puppies crawling all over. It was something to be remembered.

Linda Austin Rutledge

Without Dad
Written and Illustrated by Linda Austin Rutledge

SUMMER

Linda Austin Rutledge

Without Dad
Written and Illustrated by Linda Austin Rutledge

Summer

13

We knew when school ended it was time for great summer adventures. Living in two acres carved out of the woods our home never really was as hot as other homes. The giant oaks shaded the entire yard most of the day. We had a sandbox in the middle of the back yard that was in the sun for about three hours and that was the most we saw. The summer months were long and lazy it was a time for relaxing and reading books.

The wheat ripened in the heat of the summer and I can remember climbing in the truck load of grain and feeling the grains part as I walked back and forth until I found the perfect spot to nestle down in the grain and watch the clouds pass. We made a game of cloud watching, finding shapes in whichever cloud happened to be above us. Ships, trains and animals all floated by.

Kruegers also bailed hay in the late summer. The fields were across the road from our house. We would catch a ride on top of a full wagon of hay, ducking down as they drove into the barn. Then we would take a drink from a metal dipper in the spring well and catch a ride back home on one of the empty wagons. The bales of hay were stored for winter months to feed the cows. There was a great rope that hung from the main rafter and we could swing all the way across the barn to the other loft. The barn was an old one and the wind would always be whistling through the walls. In the barn there was always a litter of cats that kept the mouse population down and were there for us to play with.

One year we decided to set up a vegetable stand and took a card table and chairs to the roadside. We had tomatoes but needed sweet corn. Well one of us kids got the bright idea that field corn was editable so we picked field corn and sold it. Now I don't think it was done to be dishonest because we really didn't know any better. None of the buyers ever came back nor complained to us. I don't think they were very happy when they cooked it up. It had to be a pretty tough piece of corn on the cob. We made a great profit that year.

The neighbor to the south of us owned a small home on many acres. He lived in the city but would come out in the summer and plant large gardens. The biggest and best watermelon and muskmelon came from his farm. On a hot day we would walk through the woods to his backfield and sit in the hot sun eating melons. I have never had to this day a watermelon or muskmelon that tasted

Without Dad
Written and Illustrated by Linda Austin Rutledge

as sweet as those. Even the ones he brought over to us never tasted the same.

Linda Austin Rutledge

Without Dad
Written and Illustrated by Linda Austin Rutledge

FALL

Linda Austin Rutledge

Without Dad
Written and Illustrated by Linda Austin Rutledge

Fall

14

Fall would come too soon. It meant going back to school and leaving the lazy summer days behind. Mom would always buy me plaid dresses with white collars and socks to match. All the dresses were alike but the plaid color. I loved new school dresses as during the summer we each had only one pair of jeans each that we wore everyday except Monday, which was wash day. Then we put a pair of cut off shorts made from our old jeans. The dresses were a welcome change. Mom would buy us a new coat every year but I remember her having the same coat for years and years. We always came first.

We would start raking the leaves in September and not quit until November. We had great bonfires every evening, which made the raking worth while. The crickets would change their song around August and we would feel the change coming on. The large hickory trees would drop their hickory nuts and the squirrels would start gathering them up. We loved eating the nuts and would sit under the tree for hours cracking them open with two bricks.

My Dad had a beautiful shotgun and after he died mom kept it standing in the closet. When we were just little ones we took it in the back yard to shoot. It was one of the few possessions he had left to remember him by. We shot it and it knocked us off our feet. Deciding we were hunters at a very young age we went hunting. As we were walking through a field, we saw a sheriff deputy, he thought that small children should not be hunting and met us at home to warn us of the dangers of hunting. We gave up hunting for many years to come.

My brother Bill when he grew older was a great hunter. In the fall he would shoot rabbits and pheasants with my dad's shotgun. He would clean and mom would cook them up. It is surprising that we did not get lead poisoning from eating because of all the lead pellets that were still in the meat. Bill also tried taxidermy and never do I remember seeing a finished product. The basement really took on a bad odor during that time. Mom never discouraged any experiments sorry to say.

Mom would start canning tomatoes in the summer and end in the fall. She was big on tomato juice and stewed tomatoes. I ate so many tomato dishes I can't believe that I still enjoy them now. I still plant tomatoes and it would not be right if I was unable to go out and pick a fresh tomato from

Without Dad
Written and Illustrated by Linda Austin Rutledge

the garden. My second favorite was sweet peas fresh from the pod. These were only good if you were in the garden. They actually did not taste that great cooked.

Linda Austin Rutledge

Without Dad
Written and Illustrated by Linda Austin Rutledge

WINTER

Linda Austin Rutledge

Without Dad
Written and Illustrated by Linda Austin Rutledge

Winter

15

Winters in Michigan always were exciting. We knew that we would be snowed in at least two or three times. Because we had a basement full of canned fruits and vegetables we knew we wouldn't starve. I always started looking for snow before November. To the west of our house were acres and acres of open fields and to the east woods. When a great storm came it would blow into our yard hit the woods and pile snow so high we sometimes couldn't pry open the back door because of the drifts.

The crystal ice hung down from the eves too form foot long icicles, and the snow glistened in the sun. We would put so many layers of clothing on that we could hardly move. We didn't see our cousins much in the winter because the bikes were put away. We did get together to ice skate on Woodchuck Creek. Mostly we stayed home and played in the snow.

Christmas was always magical; I still remember hearing Santa's reindeers on the rooftop, later my brother admitted to throwing rocks on the roof that sounded like the real thing. Aunt Elise would bring her homemade German cookies by for us to enjoy. Aunts and uncles would bring us gifts and my Aunt Norma could always be counted on to bring me some art supplies.

We always had a fresh tree to decorate with old glass ornaments and mom had these awful red cellophane wreaths she would hang in the windows. I at a very young age decided to cut snowflakes from paper and tape to every window. It was a tradition that lasted the rest of my entire life. My Aunt Norma took one look at the beautiful snowflakes and declared me a great artist. When later asked how the snowflake tradition started I really did not want to tell anyone it was a cover-up for red wreaths.

In my lifetime two favorite gifts stand out. One year my mother won at a local store a beautiful doll. She stored it under her bed in November saving it as a gift for me. I of course found it and played secretly with it for weeks before Christmas packing it carefully back in the tissue paper lined box. Once I actually was given the doll it lost all its excitement.

The second favorite gift was a pair of new ice-skates. As we grew older Mom would tell us exactly how much money she could spend on each of us and we would pick what we wanted from the Christmas Catalog. I asked for the new ice-skates

Without Dad
Written and Illustrated by Linda Austin Rutledge

and they were the most beautiful skates I had ever seen, up until that time I had always used someone else's hand me downs.

Unlike adults we were always sad to see the ice and snow start melting it meant an end to snowmen and ice-skating and all the winter fun.

Linda Austin Rutledge

Without Dad
Written and Illustrated by Linda Austin Rutledge

THE END OF MY CHILDHOOD

Linda Austin Rutledge

Without Dad
Written and Illustrated by Linda Austin Rutledge

The end of my childhood

16

I can remember two things that stand out as the end of my childhood. First was realizing that I was a girl. Buzzy the one kid that wasn't my cousin gave me a bottle of perfume for Christmas one year. I did not realize anything unusual about it but come spring he had the nerve to tell me that he had a crush on me. Well up until that I really did not consider myself anything but one of the guys. My reaction came so quickly I did not even think. I did the only thing any self-respecting Tomboy could do. I immediately jumped him hitting him and made him take it back and say uncle. I was shocked he could think of me as a girlfriend. I disliked him for many years after and really feel bad to this day that he had to be the bearer of such bad news. After all I was a girl and one of my cousins even told me I was a very pretty girl except for my freckles. But a girlfriend UCK!

The second incident was Aunt Elise. Now I would run with the cousins all week and they never really thought of me as a girl, I was a cousin, which had no gender in our world. Well one summer day Aunt Elise took me aside and after giving me one of her great sugar cookies, told me that she thought I might be getting a little to old to be playing with the boys. I always listened to adults and took everything to heart. I thought about it for days and even though it broke my heart I knew she was right.

I started visiting my cousin, in the city. She would actually hang out on the sidewalks with friends and opened a new world of adventures none half as great as the ones I shared with my country cousins but good just the same. I remember spending the first night at her house unable to go to sleep because of the streetlights shinning in the bedroom window. I was used to only moonlight.

My City Aunt and Uncle absorbed me in just like one of their four kids. My city cousin to my wonderment-liked boys and thought of them as boyfriends. I didn't get it. Years later I found out that they could be more that just friends. I even ended up marrying one.

I was not sad to end my childhood it was just a change that came about naturally. Just as I was not sad to grow up without my Dad I thought of him every day of my life. His presence and always seemed to surround me like a guardian angel. I am sure with all my adventures someone had to be looking out for me and I feel good to think it was

Without Dad
Written and Illustrated by Linda Austin Rutledge

him. No one can remain a child forever, but we can keep the great memories. I am thankful for all that I had and for all that I did and never would I want to change one minute growing up without Dad.

THE END

ABOUT THE AUTHOR

Linda K. Austin Rutledge was born in Monroe, Michigan. She is married with three children and is the owner of "The Rutledge Agency" an investment brokerage Co. She is an artist, and is a member of the Monroe Art League. Selling paintings is her hobby.

Printed in the United States
20063LVS00001B/76-84